MW00898706

JUST A MASK

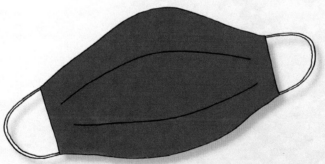

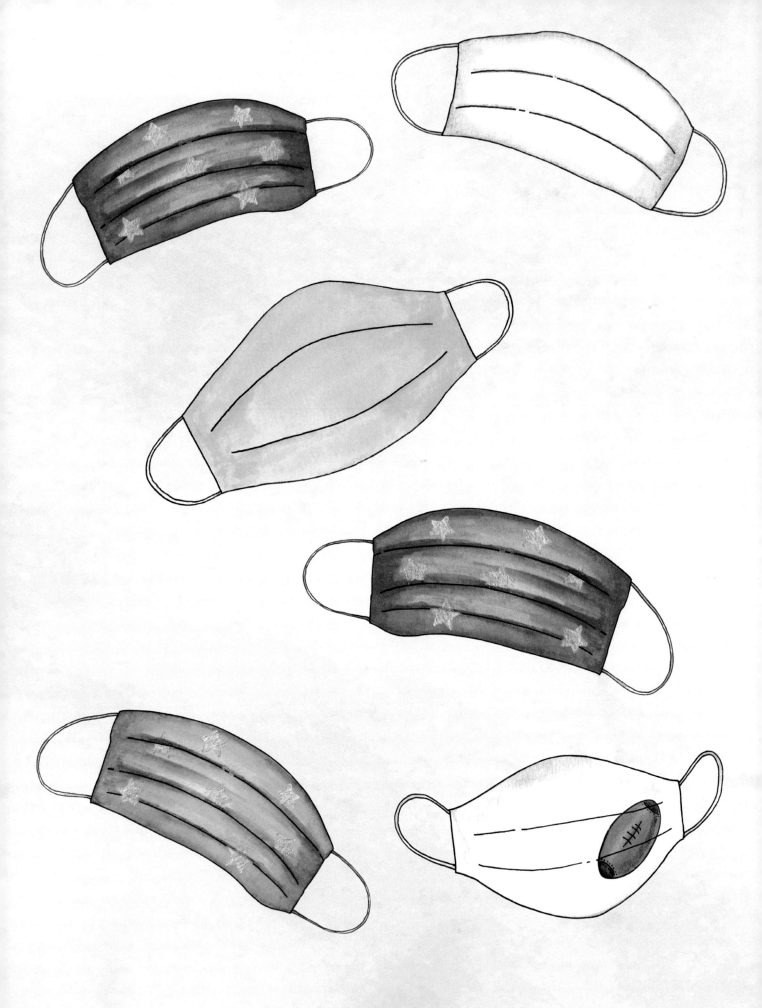

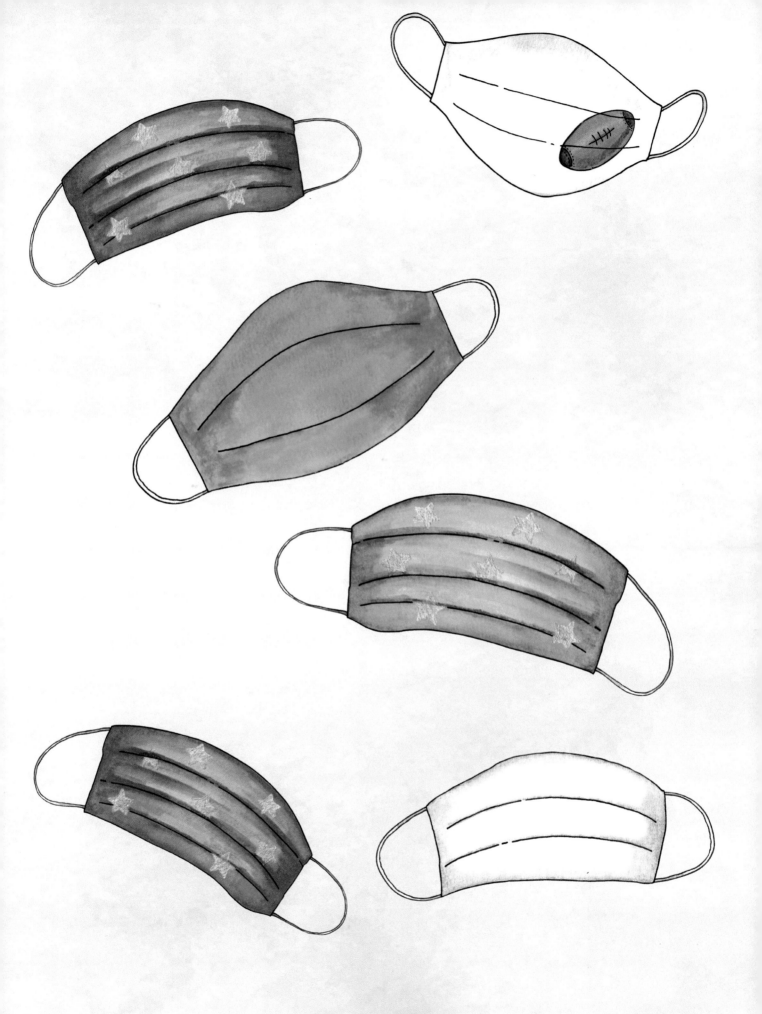

For all educators teaching during this pandemic (face-to-face, virtual, synchronous, asynchronous, hybrid, and any other way that the future may bring).

-J.B.G.

Text © 2020 by Josefina Bernal-Gurrola
Cover art and interior illustrations © 2020 by Eva Gomez
All rights reserved. Published by Wind and Rain Press.

No part of this publication may be reproduced, stored in a retrieval system, or transmitted in any form or by any means, electronic, mechanical, photocopying, recording, or otherwise, without written permission of the publisher. For information regarding permission, write to Wind and Rain Press, Attention: Permissions Department, 810 Miguel Pedraza Sr. Ct, Ysleta Sur, TX 79927.

This book is a work of fiction. Places, characters, and incidents are either the product of the author's imagination or are used fictitiously. Any resemblance to actual persons, establishments, or occurrences is coincidental. The publisher does not assume responsibility for third-party websites or their content.

Paperback ISBN: 978-1-7356287--0-7 / Hardcover ISBN: 978-1-7356287-1-4 / Ebook ISBN: 978-1-7356287-2-1

Library of Congress Control Number: 2020915947   10 9 8 7 6 5 4 3 2 1

First edition, 2020

JUST A MASK

Josefina Bernal-Gurrola

Illustrated by Eva Gomez

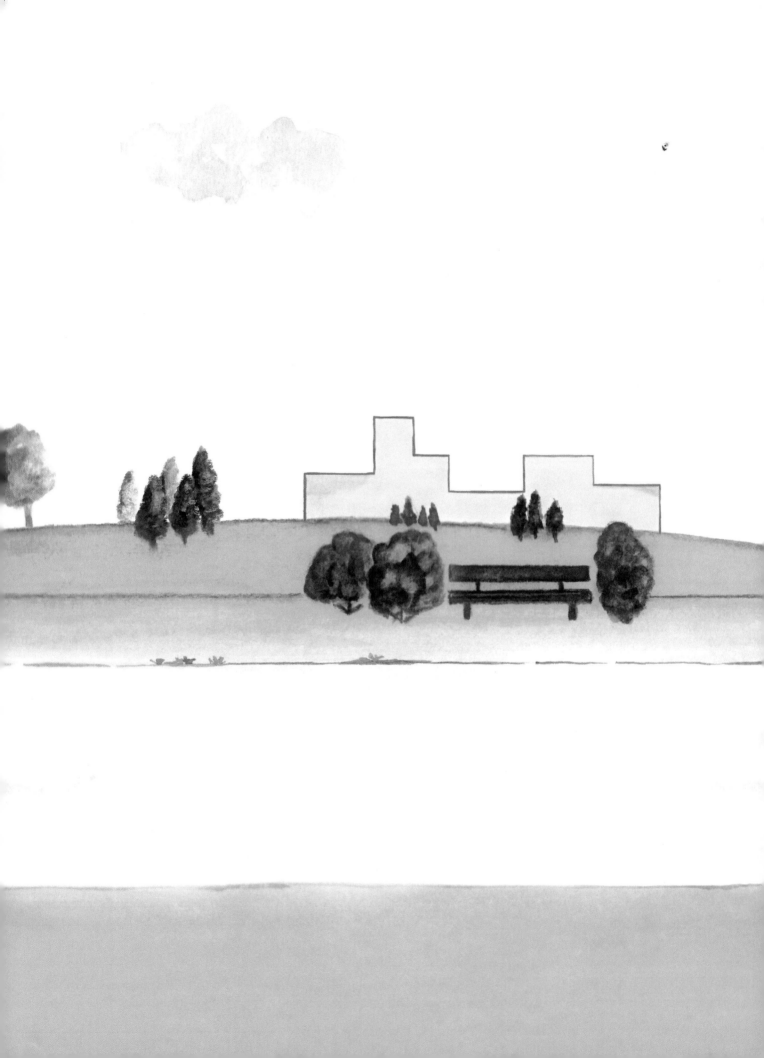

A portion of the proceeds from this book will be used to assist economically disadvantaged communities.

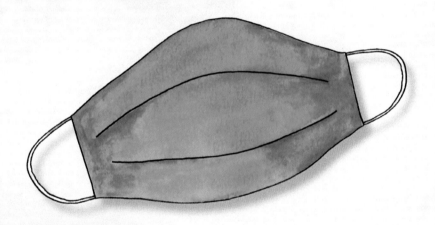

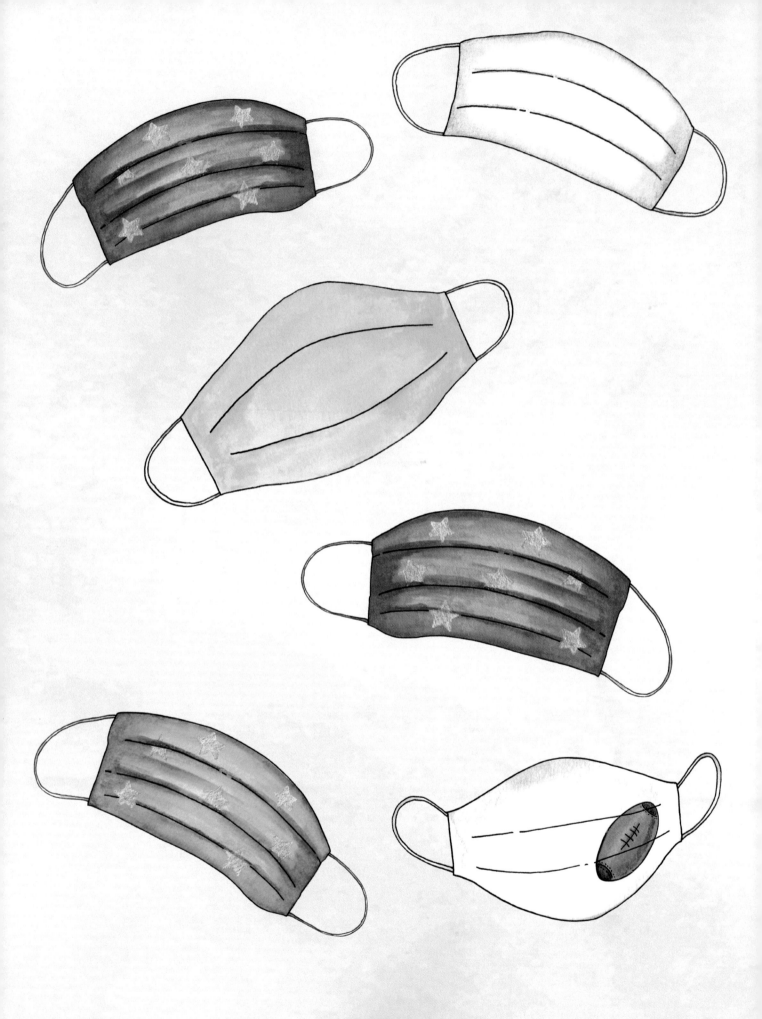

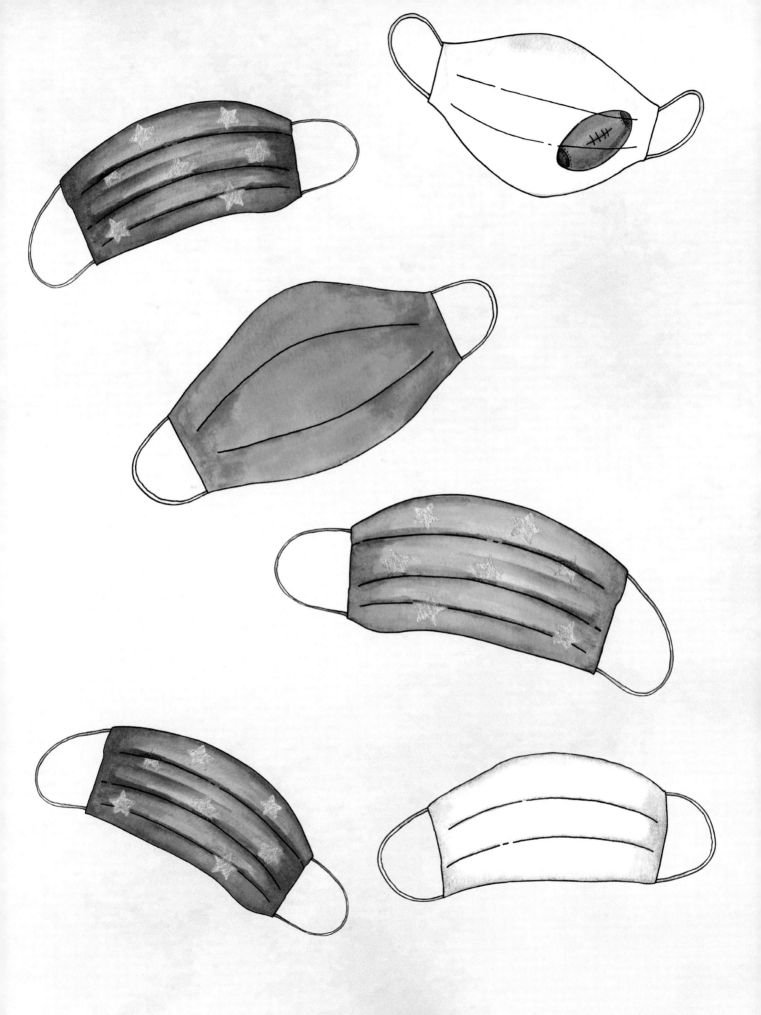

Made in the USA
Middletown, DE
21 October 2020

22465790R00018